Becoming Anastasia

Kayla Smickle

Acknowledgements

To Calisius and Darius, you motivate me to be the best mother I can be.

Thank you, Andre, you encourage me regularly and remind me to take my time, I love you dearly for that.

Thank you, Samantha, you helped me immensely at the beginning of this story and words can't express how grateful I am for your help.

To my mom, Naida, thank you for proofreading and brainstorming with me, it means the world.

To my Manifestation Goddesses, you know who you are, thank you for consistently motivating me.

Contents

Chapter 1

————◆◆◆————

Hmmm. Where to begin. Probably the best place is my last year of high school...

My name is Anastasia, I am a 17-year-old biracial girl who lives happily with her family in a small town called Mount view in Ontario, Canada.

My mother is always looking out for me, guiding me, she cares for me like no other. My father hugs me daily, tells me he loves me, and it makes me feel safe. I have two little brothers who I adore (when they are not pestering me). I like my home, my area, the community feels safe. To be frank, my life is pretty good, I don't really have any major problems or concerns that could make my head spin out of control, my parents have done a good job at protecting my brothers and I.

My life is about to change drastically. More and more the teachers and school counsellors are pushing us to "make a plan" by showing the multiple options available to us, asking us to choose our next path and determine what we want to be when we "grow up". I wonder if they understand how big a decision this will be for us? Do they understand that half of us will choose a program of study only to fail or possibly hate what we chose and drop out? Leaving us to feel inadequate, incapable of achieving lifelong goals, and deeming ourselves failures.

I don't agree with this cycle, I feel like it's a game and I'm a pawn. I have heard my mother and father speak of their college days. They followed their hearts, chased their 'hobbies' as they like to call it; worked so hard to the point of frustration and sometimes tears, only to be left in debt to the government and graduating during a recession. Hearing this did not make me want to even think about College or University for a long time but everyone seems to think you need to finish high school and go straight into a career to become an adult, it has to be done as soon as possible or you could lose interest and possibly never end up going. My parents told me that if you don't have a University Degree on your job application, you don't stand a chance of getting a well-paying job.

Given the hardship that my parents faced, they want to play a key part in my future, as in; they want to choose my courses and pay for my education. I understand where they are coming from but it doesn't feel good to me. I feel knots in my stomach every time I think about this, I don't understand why it bothers me so much but something inside feels off.

When my grandmother visits, she just plays on my ego, she'll say things like "Anastasia, you're so beautiful. Look at your perfect curls! Hourglass figure, what I wouldn't give! You should be modelling…" on and on she goes. I love her and appreciate her for the compliments but I never was into the 'spot light' I don't think I am brave enough to put myself forward and maintain confidence if others would reject me. So, even though my grandmother wants me to be a famous model, I don't think that's a right fit for me either.

I have two best friends, Jessica and Khadijah. Jessica appears to be calm and collected in her thoughts, she has a relaxed view on life and I appreciate her for that. She can make me feel like any situation can be handled without over thinking the process. Jessica has been teaching me about my intuition, she told me all the answers are there. Ask a question and you can always hear an answer she says. Jessica is my spiritual strength.

Khadijah is realistic and logical; she is great at using reasoning and research to make good decisions. She has put a lot of thought into what she plans to do next but I can see it has taken a toll on her stress level. She feels there are a lot of expectations from her family, there is no room to fail so she has to make a decision that she knows will have the most logical and reliable outcome. Khadijah is my go-to for anything practical, if I need a stern answer, she is my girl and I know I can trust her advice.

At school there is a College and University fair where students come from all over the province and try to convince us 'high schoolers' that they have the top program with the best results. It resembles a science fair, everyone walking around looking at your work and then judging it to determine the winner.

"Have you decided what you want to study Anastasia?"

"Not yet Khadijah, I am still trying to figure it out, I really don't know what I want to do. My parents are really pushing business, finance or healthcare but I am interested in film. My mom said *'pursuing your passion is not practical'*, she told me I need to do my hobbies on my own time. I feel overwhelmed."

"Well, to be honest Ana, you do have to be realistic in your choices. Most people don't make it in the entertainment industry, especially in Canada. I suggest you do some research on the most sought-after work and try to find something interesting from there. You don't want to get older and realize you can't find any work because your field is too competitive."

Of course, Khadijah had the answers, she always had the answers, she spent so much time racking her brain about the most logical route. I became silent in thought.

I felt a slight tap on my shoulder, turned around and Jessica gave me a very nice, soft hug. "Hey boo," Jess said with a slight smile on her face.

"Jess, have you made any decisions yet?" I gestured towards all the chaos of our peers frantically trying to make one of the biggest decisions of their lives.

"Honestly…no. This does not need to take up your energy at this time, when it feels right, you will know." Jessica smiled.

I felt calm but it was momentary as soon as I thought of my parents my mood changed again. "My parents want me to choose something specific, based on what they think would be best for me, and I am afraid I will not be happy with it."

"Ana, you have a strong and helpful intuition that you can use at any time, chill out and meditate about it. If you have to pay for it yourself be prepared, you can survive anything. You can take your time on this decision; it doesn't have to be immediate."

Khadijah at this point intervened, "Jess, if she waits too long to make a decision, she just gets older and it takes longer to finish school. Don't you want to be done with it as soon as possible?"

Jessica gave a slight smile and looked at me, "It's up to you boo." We went about our day and I felt uneasy the whole time.

There's information and advertising all over the school, everyone's trying to sell the superiority of their school and programs. When I get home, mom keeps asking if I made a decision or if I need help doing research on future careers. I just need a break from it. I really can't stand it. It's causing me stress, like an ache in the pit of my stomach, sometimes like uncontrollable butterflies but not the kind you feel when you are excited, it's more like a negative feeling.

I couldn't understand why this was bothering me so much, I thought maybe it was because I was afraid to fail, but fail in what? I felt like I couldn't breathe.

"Hi Ana, I'm home", mom came through the door. "How are you? How is school? I am going to shower and then we can chat in the kitchen while I cook." Mom is always on the go.

"Okay mom, school was good. I am good. Talk soon."

My brothers are 12 and 6 years old, they do not have these kinds of stresses yet, plus they have the *male* advantage so it just seems like they will always experience life easier than me. I help take care of them, I help them both do their homework and I do mine, then I have to have the 'kitchen talk' which is pretty much the daily ritual in this house.

My mother comes down the stairs and goes into the kitchen, she grabs all the ingredients she needs from the fridge and gets to work. I sit on the bar stool at the island and get ready for the conversation.

"So... how was the fair today? Anything insightful or interesting?"

I breathe deeply and pass her a brochure from one of the colleges I have some interest in.

She looks at the brochure and does not look impressed at all. She sighs and looks at me, "Ana, this is not what we talked about. I have told you before, nothing comes of any art or film school. I have already experienced this, and I don't think it would be the right choice for you. It is a competitive field where no one wants to help in that industry, especially if you're a woman."

"Yes, but mom you decided to have a baby during school, that must have added extra stress to your life." The baby of course was me.

"This is true, however I can't say it was a real mistake since you turned out to be so awesome." She looked up from cooking and smiled at me then started chopping peppers again. "That being said, I just don't want you to waste your time. So many people end up going back to school over and over again because they make the wrong decision initially. A job is a job, it's meant to give you money and provide for all of life's luxuries, if you have the right job you can spend your spare time and money on all the things you actually enjoy doing with your time like filming videos and posting them online or going out with your friends and travelling."

"Can we at least wait until dad gets home so I can see what he thinks? I feel like I could convince you two."

She sighed and said, "We will see."

I got up and started helping her with dinner.

Later, at the dinner table dad asked us how our day was, my brothers replied in one-word answers, "Good". This response always irritates my dad. I guess he just wants to hear more about our lives since he is in the office so much. He looked at me with hope in his eyes and I started to explain what I want to study.

"I know it all seems exciting, Ana, but to be honest it's not easy in the entertainment business. Your mom and I both went through it. She studied film and I, game design. The school's promised us a great deal of opportunities, not one showed up and we ended up jobless looking for any type of work we could get. You know I had to start in the warehouse and work my way up to corporate. I just want the best for you, and we don't have a lot of money to waste on different programs if you change your mind."

I looked at my dad and mom. I could see the sympathy in their eyes, but I just got frustrated and couldn't hold it in anymore, "I am so sick of you two telling me what to do! I have listened to everything you have said over and over again. May I remind you that you two decided to have a baby while in school? You obviously made it harder on yourselves, you can't take your example and keep shoving it onto me!"

My mom then chimed in, "Yes we did go through all of that and we created this roof over your head! *And* we take care of you and your brothers. We constantly do jobs we can't stand to keep you all comfortable. We work hard and sacrifice for you. Say what you want but when you get older and have to deal with all these grown up responsibilities you will understand, and my biggest hope for you is that this world doesn't break you!"

I was now looking down and I felt my stomach twitch and turn into knots. I started crying, it was almost uncontrollable. No one moved from the table except my little brother, he came over and tried to hug me, but I was so frustrated I just left the table and went to my room.

I dove head first into my bed. I was wailing, at one point I couldn't believe the noise coming out of me, I wondered if it was even me. It felt like I had no control over my body or mind. I was breathing hard and just crying. I climbed under my blanket and started praying, "God, please tell me why, why is this the way? Why is the world like this? Why is it so hard? Why do I care so much about this when there are other kids in the world in a much worse situation? Why does it hurt? Please help me, please help me", I asked repeatedly for help until I eventually fell asleep.

Chapter 2

I awoke the next day. I could feel a huge weight lifted off me, I felt much lighter. In fact, I felt extremely happy. I opened my eyes, my room was so bright. The light was streaming in from the windows and had an intense feeling of warmth like I was being held lovingly in my parents' arms.

The light suddenly started getting brighter and brighter, and the room began to fade. I was confused but at the same time I just didn't panic, I didn't feel scared at all. I felt calm.

A moment later I was standing in a garden. A big, beautiful garden. it was so green, so bright, and had so many colourful flowers. I saw long tall grass walls and big white pillars with green vines wrapped around them; it looked like an entrance. I walked towards the tall pillars and entered further into the garden. It was the perfect temperature, the sky was clear and the sun was shining on me, I could feel butterflies in the pit of my stomach.

My mind feels clear, I have no thoughts, no worries, no concerns, just living in the moment and feeling love for all the nature I was seeing in front of me. All my confusion and anger just didn't matter and didn't seem to exist here.

Where is here? I looked around and a young man who appeared to be in his thirties with dark hair and soft features presented himself. He didn't say anything, but I already knew his name. It was Gabe. He knew me, and he felt extremely familiar to me, I could feel all of this without even saying a word. Finally, he spoke, "Welcome Anastasia, I am your spirit guide, my name is Gabe."

He put out his hand to hold mine, I took his hand for a moment, I looked at this man and I could feel warmth, kindness and safety. I placed my hand back at my side and responded "Gabe, where am I?"

He replied, "You know this place. You have been here before, many times. You are here at this moment to have a glimpse of this place again, you will find the answers you are looking for."

I was comfortable with Gabe. He started walking and I followed him. We walked through the magnificent garden together in silence, but it didn't feel like silence, we could simply communicate with our minds.

I could hear myself asking, "Gabe where are you when I am not here?"

Gabe looked at me and smiled "You can hear me speak to you often, through your own voice, you call it intuition. I also speak to you through things you call coincidences and even through images or messages from other humans that connect to you. You're feelings are a clear indication of when you can hear me the most and when you are at your highest frequency of vibration."

We sat for a moment on a white rock next to a pond. The pond was clear and I could see little fish, gold, purple and blue swimming around contently in the water.

I had a feeling I would be leaving the garden soon. "Gabe, I feel so good inside, do I have to leave?"

Gabe smiled "It's always like that for you. It's hard to leave but you know you want to. You love to experience contrast. I have noticed you have some resistance in your human form, hence the anger and confusion you are experiencing. I brought you back here because you are a creator, and it is what you love to do. I want you to experience an alternate reality, as some may call it. I believe you should see what it would be like if everything were easy for you. I am hoping you will understand that the contrast you will experience in your life is what makes you a powerful human."

"What is contrast Gabe?"

"Contrast is that of which you do not desire but molds you into who you are, which causes you to create."

I didn't get it. I was trying to understand but it was confusing, nonetheless.

Gabe stood up and gestured for me to take his hand once more. I took his hand and followed him, he led me to a brown wooden door. The door was standing alone, almost floating in the air, nothing behind it. I knew I was going to step through this door and see what was on the other side. I looked at him, "See you around Gabe." I put my hand on the doorknob, turned it and stepped through the bright light to the other side.

Chapter 3

On the other side of the door was my home. I was back in my room and I thought for a moment it was a dream, until I looked around and everything was different. My room was organized very neatly, and I had many books.

I cleaned myself up and went downstairs. No one was there, the whole house was rearranged, it was almost empty except for some furniture here and there. I went to the kitchen, where I can usually find my mom and dad around this time of day. They were not there so I headed outside.

Outside is sunny and bright, no clouds in the sky and the streets were full of people. I noticed the houses seemed smaller but sturdier, almost like they were made from the Earth. I walked for about 30 seconds and saw my mom, dad and two brothers just having fun, they were playing tag in a grassy area. As I looked around everyone appeared to be happy and peaceful, I can already see this place is different. I could sense a calm within me. I felt satisfied.

I ran over to my family. "Tag! You're it!" said my youngest brother. He ran off laughing and I started to chase him, laughing as well.

My parents brought out a blanket for us to sit on and we sat underneath a big beautiful willow tree that I hadn't paid much attention to before. As I looked around, I saw many more trees, more than had been there before, well-aged and full of wisdom. I realized I never really appreciated the nature that surrounds us, but now I see it clearly, I see the big willow tree.

My dad passed me some watermelon, it was the tastiest watermelon I ever ate, it was red in colour with dark seeds.

"Dad, this is amazing! It's so juicy and sweet!"

Dad looked at me approvingly.

"It does taste pretty good, our neighbour did an amazing job with this batch, I have been anticipating them." He smiled and bit into a piece.

We all sat together under the tree and ate and laughed. I hadn't felt at ease like this since I was a child, I felt a blanket of warmth wrapped around me.

I looked to my mom who had my brothers laying their heads in her lap. "Mom, I hope you're not upset with me for what I said the other night. I was just frustrated. I'm sorry. We can look at some options together for school later on if you like."

My mother looked at me for a moment like I was crazy and said, "Ana, you can do whatever you want. Do you want to travel anywhere? Read more books? teach yourself a new trade? It is up to you. What do you choose to do with your time?"

I was confused, "But mom, what about money? How can I do anything or whatever I want without money?"

She laughed, "Ana, what is money? I don't understand this question, what an interesting word."

I started to feel a bit perplexed, I stood up and decided I needed to do some exploring in this new reality. I told my mom and dad I was going to see my friends, to which they responded, "Have fun." No questions asked, I was able to leave without any interrogation whatsoever. I was starting to really like this place.

I thought to myself *"Gabe, this place is amazing."* To which I responded to myself *"Enjoy it while you can."*

I met up with Jessica and Khadijah at the park. They were smiling and each gave me a big hug.

"Hey boo", Jessica smiled. "How are you? What should we do today?"

My friends seemed different, both seemed extremely relaxed almost as if time just stood still, there was no rush, no urgency to leave and be on time for some sort of engagement. We could just be in this moment, we did not have to think about later on or tomorrow. There was no nervous energy anymore.

Khadijah replied to Jessica's question, "Let's go on the train and travel for a while. I have been wanting to see new places. I hear there is a part of the world that is hot all the time and there is another part of the world that is cold all the time. I'd like to visit where it is hot."

When she said this, I knew I needed more answers as to where I was and how this place worked. I proceeded to ask my friends multiple questions.

"How come we don't have money?"

"I don't know what that is." Khadijah replied.

"It's something you give people in exchange for food, clothing, homes. Basically, if you want anything from someone you need to give them money first."

Jessica said "That is the strangest thing I have ever heard. We just give each other what we need. If I need some milk from a cow I just take it, with love of course. Sometimes my neighbour brings me over some clothing she sews. I plant vegetables near my home, once it is all grown I like to take as much as I can to the neighbours around me, and they do the same."

This sounded too good to be true, "What if I want a big juicy steak right now?"

Khadijah responded "We all wait for the cows to mature before we indulge in the meat. All of us usually get together and plan a date and time when we will put down the cow and share the meat. It's a fun little celebration." She smiled.

I had never seen my friends so content. Everyone just worked together in harmony. *What do I do here?* I thought.

My inner voice replied, *why don't you take this time to see as much as you can?*

As much as I can? I thought.

"How about a library? Is there one around here?" I asked.

My friends led me down the street and we stopped at a house, it is what we would consider the size of a mansion without all the gold trim and little luxuries like exquisite molding. The house had big grey and white bricks on the exterior and a wood door. However, I noticed that it looked unfinished, it looked like there was construction pending at the side of the home, like a new home was being built. I pointed it out to my friends.

"Why is that part of the house open?"

"It's like that so we can keep expanding it. Everyone adds information often. Many of the books are made from people who have already ascended. We read their books to gain more knowledge." Khadijah said as she was leading us into the house.

I went in, I looked around, there were shelves upon shelves of books. Majority of the shelves and furniture in the home was made out of fresh wood, there was a natural pine smell. The books were organized, I could see books were placed on the shelves in alphabetical order. I pulled a book down off the shelf, it was titled *Crista Melody*. I opened the first page and started reading, this was someone's life written for everyone to read, it was a memoir.

"Hi." A voice said behind me; I jumped, startled and spun around to see this boy smiling at me, he had a gorgeous smile. "Hi" I said while smiling.

"I am Lorenzo, it is my pleasure to meet you." He held out his hand.

"I'm Anastasia, Ana for short, nice to meet you as well." I put my hand in his and he held it for a moment, I felt a surge in my body.

"How would you like to spend the day together?"

My mind started racing, he's so forward and direct, so handsome. He looked about 18 years old, with dark brown eyes and olive skin. I felt like I just met the man of my dreams. *What is wrong with me?* I thought. I had so many butterflies and a thought came to me; *it's good to feel love.*

Chapter 4

<hr>

Lorenzo and I didn't just spend one day together, we spent a few days together, just talking and walking around, gathering food, feeding each other and sharing food with others. I felt complete satisfaction.

Lorenzo is the first boy that I felt attracted to. We have great chemistry, but I keep getting the feeling that something is missing. Everything is so perfect, there is no anger or better yet, no negative emotions. I don't know why but I was feeling like I might actually miss the drama of my life before, but I just brushed it off. I brushed it off everyday telling myself that I was crazy, this place is perfect.

Lorenzo and I were inseparable for a whole week and then he asked me a question "Ana, let's go to my birthplace, I want to show you how different it is. I think you will love it there. Different food grows in my area, we have olives and grapes and the weather is just perfect. I would also love to show you the salt water."

"You mean the sea, right?"

"Is that salt water? If so, then yes, I like that word 'sea' have you already seen it?"

"A long time ago I went on vacation with my parents but I am sure it is nothing like what I will be seeing with you. I'd love to go."

I went home and grabbed a bag with only a few items because everything is pretty much available to you here. If you need a change of clothes knock on anyone's door and they will give it to you. If you need food or somewhere to sleep, it is the same thing. People just give and share and live in complete harmony.

As I was leaving my house I found my parents outside under the willow tree, relaxing and holding hands. "Mom, dad, can I go see where Lorenzo lives?"

I still felt that my parents were going to start yelling at me and telling me that I can't go anywhere, that I was too young and the world is a dangerous place, but instead I received the following;

"Have fun."

Have fun? What do they mean *have fun?*

"So…you are letting me go with a boy I just met to swim in salt water, which I am assuming is a long way from here and you may not hear from me for a long time and you're telling me to *have fun?*"

My mom looked at me and smiled, "Yes Ana, have fun. We know you will be fine, there is so much beautiful things to see and experience in this life, I want you to enjoy it all. I'll see you when you get back and you can tell me all about it."

I hugged them both and turned to walk away. "We love you!" my parents said, I suddenly started feeling excited, for the first time in this reality I was starting to feel free, uncontrolled by anyone or any system. The excitement took complete control over me, I grabbed Lorenzo's hand and started running through the street towards the train station. This is freedom, the option to do whatever I want, be whoever I want to be and there is no one here to judge me or tell me I am wrong.

Chapter 5

L orenzo and I jumped on the train and we were off. Our journey was long, we stopped in many different areas and Lorenzo would show me around. I was seeing new things; different foods grew in different areas and the clothing was different as well. Even the homes would change depending on what the Earth provided in each region. People could understand each other, there were no language barriers. We all seemed to be connected, even if someone spoke in a different language, I knew what they were saying and they knew what I was saying, it was my intuition, constantly guiding me. All people we came across were loving and kind. I truly had nothing to worry about.

We were on the train and then got on a plane for the final bit of our travel. The trains and planes were designed completely differently from ours, they both ran off solar power. The train is much slower than what I was used to. No one is in a rush to get anywhere which made this form of transportation to be acceptable. I noticed that the train was not run by one person, it seemed once we reached a check point a new person would check out the train for maintenance and move it forward. Lorenzo told me the people who did this were the ones who helped build it.

At first, I was a bit impatient. "Lorenzo, how long does it take to get where you live exactly?"

"Well, that depends. I like to stop and visit with friends along the way, I don't see the purpose in moving too fast. Look how beautiful everything is! There are so many different foods to try as well. We will get there when we get there."

"Okay" I said with a smile, which I started to feel may be fake, but I quickly fixed my thoughts and made myself get excited. I know that I must take advantage of all I am seeing and doing right now in this moment. Also, I really was enjoying the company of a very handsome young man as well.

We took a plane for the middle part of our journey, at first, I did not feel safe at all but Lorenzo and the pilot did not seem worried. The plane was thin and sleek and could only hold three to four people, it too ran off solar power. The plane ride was fun, Lorenzo and the pilot talked to me, they made me laugh and I just knew I would be ok.

After what felt like was months, Lorenzo took my hand and said "We are here" and we stepped off the plane.

Lorenzo led me towards a beach. It was the sea, we made it. I could see many people and children laughing and splashing in the water. As I got closer and closer I started to feel tightness in the pit of my stomach. Everyone was naked.

I stopped walking. Lorenzo didn't notice and pulled me a little but turned around to look at me as soon as he felt the resistance.

"Ana, what's wrong?"

"Everyone is naked." I knew this was going to be a tough challenge for me.

"Of course! There is no other way to swim or bathe. Let's go! I am so excited, I have been dreaming about coming here with you and now we are here."

Lorenzo started moving closer and closer to the sea. As we got closer he started taking off his clothes. He was gorgeous. I felt ashamed for feeling the way I felt about him but as I looked around I could see everyone's faces and bodies. No one was looking at us, no one was looking at me. Everyone was laughing, focused on what they were doing. I took a deep breath and thought *'let's do this.'*

My clothes came off and Lorenzo and I ran into the water. Laughing, I said "I feel so free! This water is so warm and clear, oh my gosh it is beautiful Lorenzo! I love it."

He smiled and in the water, we shared our first, very passionate kiss.

After our day at the beach Lorenzo took me to his home. It was a small house made from wood. He had a kitchen, bathroom and two bedrooms. The bed was nice, it was very comfortable.

"Lorenzo, what is this bed made out of?"

"I was able to gather some wool and feathers, I took it to my neighbour, Mary, who likes to put beds together for people. She's really good at it and clearly has mastered the craft."

I laid down on the bed and he came beside me and laid next to me. His hand touched mine, he looked deep into my eyes. "I love you, you mean very much to me and I would love us to stay connected for as long as we can."

My stomach was dancing. "I love you too. You have made me very happy." I didn't understand what he meant by *'as long as we can'* but I am ready to take the next step with him. We started kissing, our bodies became in sync with each other. He touched me in places that made me feel good and I did the same for him. We exploded with pleasure at the same time and I had never felt anything so good.

Chapter 6

———◆◆◆———

I was getting used to the world as it was. I called my parents and brothers every so often and we always had great conversations, with no worry or fear. I checked in on Jessica and she was already starting a family back home. Khadijah was travelling everywhere, she had to call me every time she moved. I was feeling it was time to figure out how I could contribute to this new reality, I felt I needed something else, I needed to start a project, if it were the way it was before I would be in school right now working towards a career.

After about a year, Lorenzo and I were growing plenty of food; we had an apple tree, strawberries, avocados, a nearby flock of sheep to tend to and received milk and wool to produce some of our favourite food and clothing.

Something in me was missing. I laid awake in bed and turned to Lorenzo, "Lorenzo, do you ever feel like something is missing? A feeling of emptiness?"

He replied, "I am not sure of this feeling you are referring to. I feel excited every day, is this the feeling you are referring to?"

I sighed, "No, it's ok, get some rest. Love you."

He smiled at me, "I love you too."

The next day I was taking a stroll around the area as I sometimes did, to think and reflect. Lately I have been reflecting more on my past. About how I would feel negative emotions but find a way to overcome them. I was unsure if I was missing the way I used to live, but I couldn't have, everything was perfect in this reality.

I was doing my daily rounds, saying hello to all my neighbours, when I heard a thump and some grunting noise, almost as if someone fell over and couldn't get up. The sound came from the back of one of the homes. I heard a man's voice he spoke angrily but in a muffled tone, "Fuck this shit." I almost wanted to laugh, I felt something I hadn't felt in a long time.

"Hello", I said. I looked down at this young man, he looked about my age. He had chocolate skin like my father. He had an angry look on his face, something I hadn't seen in a long time. He was sitting on the ground with a bag in his hand, it looked like it was leather, probably made out of sheep skin, many people did that when animals died, you can make water bottles and other sorts. He put it to his mouth and drank. I figured it was water.

He looked up at me, "Do you want some?"

I looked at him and I felt like I knew this look from before, but it didn't frighten me, I said "Yea, sure."

He passed me the skin, I put it to my mouth and tasted wine. Lorenzo and I had indulged in some before, maybe just a glass or two, it wasn't really a thing here, it just didn't seem necessary, everybody is high on life.

"Thanks, I only had this in my previous life." I am not sure why I said that, I hadn't mentioned an alternate life to anyone.

He looked at me wide eyed and said enthusiastically, "You too? So, you are like me. Well! Let's chop it up a bit. Join me, we can drink some wine and talk about the good days," he was grinning but I could sense some hurt. "I have loads of this shit at my place, let's go." He grabbed my hand and we started walking towards what I assumed to be his home. He was smiling and excited, like a kid in a candy store for the first time.

As he was leading me to his home, I had a feeling of familiarity, I felt completely comfortable even though he was like me, from a place of strife and worry.

"You're gonna love this place! I have loads of wine! We are going to have so much fun! I haven't been able to express myself properly since I got here."

He was looking at me and with so much excitement. I started to get excited. "Wait, I never got your name?", he looked at me and with the most beautiful big smile I had ever seen he said "Noah."

Chapter 7

He lead me into his home, it was small but cute. He had his kitchen, living room and bedroom all in one space, there was a wool carpet on the floor and a fireplace near the bed. There was a separate room down a hall which I assumed was the bathroom. It was simple and I loved it. "My name is Anastasia by the way."

He walked to the kitchen and grabbed two glasses from the cupboard. He grabbed some more wine which was on a shelf in a jar and we sat at a small wooden table for two. He placed the glasses and wine down on the table and pulled out a chair, gesturing me to sit down. He smiled enthusiastically and said "Anastasia is a beautiful name, it's Russian right? Are you mixed?" he sat down and started pouring the wine.

I replied in a soft tone "Yes, my dad is Jamaican and my mom is Canadian with Russian descent."

As he was pouring the wine, he noted "Nobody talks about their family roots here, they don't have any, we are all one, which can be a good thing clearly…but I do miss having old conversations." After pouring he pushed my glass towards me. "I miss getting to know someone, it's like a fun mystery to solve, unlike now, you know exactly who people are here and their intentions. Here it's all the same, everyone is happy, not much of a story to tell except in the library where they share inventions and such."

I looked at him "What about you? Where was your family from?"

He exclaimed "American, baby! From Detroit, Michigan." Noah's face changed and he looked at me intently, "I have been stuck here for two years now. I want to go back."

I was looking at him like he was crazy, "Why? Why would you want to go back? Don't you remember all the pain? All the anger and hunger? People were racist, rapists and just simply awful! The system was so corrupt! I do miss some things but this, this place is bliss."

Noah calmed himself and appeared to become somber. "I know why you might feel this way now, but it has become difficult for me to understand who I am. I don't feel like me anymore. Yes, it was awful and some moments were extremely difficult, but now I don't know my purpose. I don't know why I even live." Noah started to get angry, "I had already lost everything before I came here. My best friend was killed in front of me, my mom died from stress! My dad is nowhere to be found. I even tried looking for him in this reality and I can't find him. I don't know what to do with myself!"

Tears silently fell down his cheeks. I hadn't seen this much pain in so long, or it feels like a long time. Not long ago I too had my own struggles and pain, but nothing like what Noah went through. And even though I could never understand what he was going through I felt for him. I wanted to comfort him, let him know everything would be alright. I got up from the table and hugged him, held him in my arms and he was silent for a moment, then reached for his wine as he tried to compose himself.

Noah wiped his face and looked at me, "Everything is perfect so what do I do to become better? How do I create opportunity for growth? Being here makes me feel like everything I went through was for nothing. It feels like there are no challenges."

"I can't answer that Noah. I genuinely thought at one point that my stresses were difficult but when I compare them to yours, they seem so minimal. I had to deal with trying to decide what to do with the rest of my life, what school to choose, and how to make my parents proud. You have been through so much more hardship that I will never understand."

Noah looked at me, almost with some relief in his eyes, "Regardless of what you have been through, you are compassionate, and it has made you who you are and I think I really like who you are." He gave me his big smile and passed me a glass of wine.

The rest of the day we talked, we laughed, we told stories about home. We spoke about our spirit guides, his was a female named Alya. He told me he could hear her voice often but many times he chose to ignore it.

Noah and I had such a great time; our conversations went from high to low. He told me all about his mom, how they lived, and how his best friend had been shot by a stray bullet and died. All the things a child should not have to see, he had seen. The more he talked, the more I admired him. I was so impressed with how beautiful his soul was even though he had every right to be angry. He enjoyed listening to me. He liked hearing about my parents and brothers; it brought a smile to his face. He told me I gave him hope.

We had spoken so much that day, I completely lost track of time. It had become dark already. I had never had much alcohol before so I started to feel a bit dizzy, "I should probably get back to my home but I think I am tipsy." I could hear my speech somewhat slurred as I spoke to Noah, I was more likely drunk than tipsy but I didn't want to expose myself to him.

He replied, "I know that I could walk you home and I know these streets are safe, but for my sake please feel free to take my bed, you need rest and I can see you home in the morning." He was sincere and I knew in my heart I could trust him, so I took his bed and went to sleep, Noah slept on the floor next to me.

Chapter 8

The next day I woke up with a slight headache and a nice aroma. I looked over and Noah was in his kitchen making food. "Good morning, I don't know what you are chefing up but it smells delicious."

Noah looked up excited to see I was awake, "Trust me, it's just what the doctor ordered! I have the water set up for you and some mint and a toothbrush," he gestured to his bathroom. "Feel free to help yourself to anything else."

I got up and walked to the bathroom. I went inside, there was some fresh olive oil to the side, I was able to apply some to my hair and brush it through, my curls looked vibrant. I washed myself, brushed my teeth and for some reason I took extra care to get myself ready and look nice for Noah. I started to realize I was trying to impress him, then I felt a bit guilty.

I came out of the bathroom. Noah was sitting at the table, the food was placed and set for me to join. He heard me open the door, spun around to look at me eagerly, smiled at me and pulled the chair to offer me a seat. I looked at him and couldn't help but smile, I could tell my smile was so big and I toned it down immediately and said "thank you."

We were eating and I could tell he wanted to say something but I felt some guilt in the pit of my stomach. I started thinking about Lorenzo, but I already knew I felt something stronger for Noah, something I haven't felt before. I gestured with my fork to the eggs and bacon Noah made me, "This is really good," I said. "I guess this is a testament to you always having to cook for yourself, it's amazing, thank you."

Noah smiled, he seemed happy for the approval. "You look beautiful by the way. Such a natural beauty." He lightly touched my face.

I blushed, I could feel the heat rush to my face, I smiled at him, "You aren't too bad yourself." He smiled and we ate.

After breakfast, I helped him clean up, we washed the dishes and chatted, we were in sync with one another.

"Do you have any plans today Anastasia? I mean, since we are free now to do what we please and live off the land I would assume you are available to sight see with me?" There was a tone in his voice, almost accusingly but I thought I must be hearing what was not there.

I thought for a moment that maybe I should check in with Lorenzo so I replied, "I need to go back home and I can come right back, just want to check in on some sheep."

He looked at me deep in my eyes and said, "Or maybe your friend is who you need to check in on?"

I looked surprised and I said, "How did you know?"

He smiled and I was relieved, "I have seen you and him around. I thought you two looked cute but also I knew something was different about you and then yesterday you approached me and now I know what it was I saw in you." He proceeded to take my hands into his and said, "I don't know why we are here, but I know we are connected. We both need to figure this out and I think we should be doing it together. My voice, the one I rarely try to listen to, is telling me you're the one."

My heart started beating so fast and he hugged me, I did not say a word. I just hugged him back; I felt so safe and secure.

I went on my way and couldn't stop smiling, I had butterflies in my stomach. I went to my home. I saw Lorenzo in the field tending to the crops. He looked so strong and handsome. He stood up and smiled at me. I came closer, we hugged and shared a kiss.

"Anastasia, my love." He held my hands in his.

My smile faded and I started to speak extremely fast, "I have to tell you something…I met someone, he really understands me, we have a lot in common and I feel I need to find some answers, I would like to spend some time with him."

Lorenzo's expression did not change, "That is wonderful!"

I looked at him and he did not seem upset or distraught at all. His reaction made me feel a bit irritated, my mind started running wild, why didn't he seem upset at all? Why wasn't he jealous or even a bit nervous about this. "Lorenzo, are you ok with this? I may be gone for a while. It could be days, even weeks, what if forever?" I could feel myself getting upset, something I hadn't felt in a long time.

He hugged me and looked at me, "My love, I love you unconditionally with no exceptions. I am happy with any way you want to live and be. You can come to me anytime you like and I will be here to love you. You can have friends and lovers, anyone who makes you feel good. You are not mine to hold onto."

We were silent for a moment and I realized this is the reality I live in now, there are no conditions to our love. When you love someone, you should let them be who they are, we do not have to compete or prove to one another that we love them. I realized in this moment that Lorenzo taught me how to be calm, to have confidence in myself and to just let things be as they are and not try to control the situation.

I could hear my inner voice, Gabe, he was speaking to me, telling me it was a good thing to allow myself to be happy. I did not need to feel sad or guilty. I am allowed to be me with no apologies. I had to admit it though, I don't know if I liked this. I don't know if I liked how easily Lorenzo let me go. I think I like it more if someone fights for me rather than letting me go without question.

This made me realize my decision was good, I realized that I wanted a little chaos, more so than I thought I did.

Lorenzo and I said goodbye, he kissed me sweetly, he said "I will keep you in my heart and hopefully see you again my love."

"Goodbye Lorenzo" I said half smiling, I turned around and started skipping with excitement to catch up with Noah. I shouted out to the sky "Bring on the chaos!" I hadn't felt this way in a long time.

As I got close to Noah's home I could sense something was amiss. His door was open. I looked inside and I could see the home in disarray. It was like he trashed the place while I was gone. "Noah?, Noah!" I looked frantically around and found him on the floor next to his bed.

Noah awoke and looked at me dreary, "You actually came back? What for? Can't you tell I'm a mess? I bet life was perfect for you." He said this to me accusingly. He stood up, he was a bit wobbly but held himself steady, "I mean, who in their right mind would even drink the way I am drinking in a perfect fucking world? The world we all hoped and prayed for most our life, a world of peace, a home like this? What the fuck is going on with me?!" He sat on his bed and held his head. I slowly walked towards him, sat down beside him and held him. He needed me, and I didn't completely understand it yet, but I needed him too.

Noah let me hold him and we eventually switched positions, I was now in his arms, we slept for hours until morning.

Chapter 9

Noah woke up feeling better and eager to go. It was as if he had a new spark of hope in him. "Anastasia, I apologize for the way I acted yesterday. I don't know what came over me, I really am trying to be better. Do you still want to come with me? See as much as we can, while we can?"

I started to feel excited again, I hadn't felt excited for anything in a while and I jumped up eager to start the journey. "Let's get 'er done." I said in an Southern accent, he laughed at me and said "nerd." We smiled at each other and got ready for a new phase in our lives.

We left his home, we started the journey by train, when the train stopped we would grab some food from the locals and when we got back on the train we would drink some wine. We were having fun, almost like a never-ending vacation. I believe we had made it to Greece and chose to stay a while; we made more wine, danced, learned how to paint, built a home, and checked out the local library to read about other people's experiences. We had all the time in the world to do whatever we wanted, we could go from continent to continent at any moment, build new homes, leave them, or even sometimes we found a home already built that we could claim temporarily. We met so many people and we learned a lot together.

Noah and I started to become very close during this time. We became extremely intimate, it was nothing like what I had with Lorenzo, this intimacy with Noah was extremely passionate. Sometimes overwhelming but in a beautiful way.

We lived like this for 2 years, travelling and enjoying our time together, we had been to many places in the world. We decided to take a trip to Noah's old home to see if we could find any familiar faces from his past.

He showed me the area he grew up, he told me "It didn't look like this before. There was garbage all over the place, the homes were run down. Everyone is just so happy now."

He showed me the spot where he saw his friend murdered from a stray bullet. We even went by the site where the police station used to be, Noah cried, "I see this now, how it all could have been and I just feel pissed! All these things that I hated and people I loved are now gone. I get so confused Ana, I am very happy with you here, I just get fucking angry sometimes. Why couldn't it have been like this before?"

We hugged and I said, "I know what you mean, it is upsetting to know that we could have a world like this but were deprived from it all. A place of no stress, worries, judgement or financial concerns, no more pressure or depression. I am deeply sorry for all that you lost." We kissed, held hands and walked back to the home we were staying in.

After a few days we decided to travel to Ontario to see my family and hometown.

It is fall now and all the leaves were turning orange and red. I was excited to be back home, I wanted to see my mom and dad and my brothers, I missed them. As we walked from the train station to my parents home I could see Noah looking around. He seemed happy. We walked up to my home, the door was painted blue. As we stopped at the door to knock, Noah said "I like it here" he smiled at me. "I really like this place, I like the area, it's nice. Did it look like this before?"

"Honestly, not much has changed. I just noticed the houses are smaller, people are nicer, and I notice a lot more nature surrounds me."

I looked at him adoringly, "maybe we could set up some roots for a while?"

He looked at me and smiled but did not respond.

I didn't understand why, but I would soon come to know that there was so much more going on with Noah that I hadn't realized. I knocked on the door and my youngest brother swung it open. "Ana! I am so happy to see you!" He hugged me tight and then turned to Noah "You must be Noah, Ana has told us about you when she calls. I've been excited to meet you." He gave Noah a big hug. We went inside and my parents and other brother were there to greet us with open arms, I could feel all the love in that one room.

We had a good time in my hometown, we spent time gardening, reading and hanging out with my parents and brothers.

Sometimes we would take a blanket out to my favourite tree, it was the big willow tree near my home, we would bundle up and read or just look at the sunset. However, as the days went on I could see Noah's face changing. His glow was fading. I couldn't ignore it. One evening I asked, "Noah what's wrong? I can tell something is very different with you lately. Please tell me, you can tell me how you are feeling."

Noah was relaxing on the bed, he looked at me, touched my chin softly, kissed my forehead and said, "I love you, I truly do. You have changed me and I feel like I have become a stronger and better man because of it. I would never regret these moments I have had with you. I cherish every moment. Please always know, whatever happens to us I will fight my way to find you." He was holding my face and kissed me, then held me for a moment before turning on his back on the bed to stare up at the ceiling.

I felt twisting knots in my stomach. *What kind of answer is that?* It made me feel confused and scared. "Noah, whatever is going on, I want you to know that you make me feel safe, you make me feel secure, I love you and I want us to keep living in this world together." Noah gestured to me by opening his arms for me to come lay on the bed with him. I crawled into his arms, he wrapped them around me and we slept.

That morning I woke to birds chirping and the sun shining on my face. I slowly opened my eyes and looked around the room. Noah was not there. I abruptly got up, I could feel something was not right and I started frantically searching the house and calling his name. I ran outside. I asked some neighbours if they had seen him, they had not.

I knew what happened, I knew in my heart the exact answer. I called out, "Gabe! Gabe, please help me. I need your help." In that moment the brown wooden door presented itself to me. I was nervous, but even more determined to find Noah. I opened it without a second thought, without hesitation.

Chapter 10

I was back in the garden. Gabe was standing there, I could hear him in my heart, this time he did not speak directly to me but I heard him inside me say *"It is time."* I spoke out loud to Gabe, "I am ready to go back now, I know that's where Noah went and I don't think I could stay here without him."

Gabe nodded.

The light started getting brighter and I heard Gabe say, "Never forget the feelings of satisfaction, love and butterflies." When he said this it made me smile, for a long moment I forgot about what I had just lost.

I awoke, I was back in my room. I felt knots in my stomach, it felt like I had woken up the day after the night I fought with my parents. I looked at the calendar hanging on my wall. I was back at the exact morning I originally left.

I was feeling awful. I brushed my teeth, got dressed and tried my best to put myself together, I said good morning to my parents and ran out the door. I was thinking of Noah. I started running down the street, with no destination in mind, I just felt like running. I ran till my breath gave out, and then headed back. I stopped at the big willow tree, it was once our tree, I sat under it and I started to cry. It was uncontrollable, my emotions were overwhelming me. I had not felt like that in a long time. I felt suffocated. I tried to take deep breaths to calm the hysteria I was feeling.

I started to calm down. I had to speak to someone, but the only person who would understand is myself; I had only myself to talk to in this moment. "Why did he leave me? Why would he want to leave what we had to come back here, to this shit?!"

I was silent for a moment and then answered myself, "You know why. You know he wanted to survive the life he already lived, he didn't want to move on knowing it all could have been prevented. He wanted to come back and fight. There is honour in that."

A few tears came down my cheek at the realization of this, "I understand but I still wish we could have done it together."

I stayed at the tree for a few hours before heading back home.

Chapter 11

The next couple of months felt like hell. I missed being able to leave and go wherever I wanted, I missed the freedom. I couldn't just walk out the front door and travel across the country with nothing in my wallet. I had to make a decision; what would I study? Who would I become? Every day I felt the world was full of shit. I felt it was all a lie and nothing made me happy anymore. I could be in a place of no judgment or restrictions, I could be with Noah, we could be free.

Every time dad watched the news I could see and hear of. all the sadness in the world: police brutality, racism, systematic racism, child abuse, murder, and talks of war. It disgusted me, just knowing what I knew was torture. I thought of Noah often, sometimes I hated him for leaving me, leaving our love in the world we met in. There were other times when I felt closer to him, I sometimes thought, *this is what Noah was talking about, this is why it was so hard to accept the freedom, all the struggle had to have a reason.* I realized it was hard for him to accept everything he went through, all his loss and trauma had to lead him to a point in his life where he could make a difference, he wanted justice and I could respect that now.

I woke up every day feeling confused and not knowing what to do. My parents were concerned, they called Khadijah and Jessica to come cheer me up. They wanted them to convince me to sign up for University but I couldn't be bothered. I felt nothing, I felt empty, I didn't even care about the passions I once had.

My friends ended up being accepted into school, Khadijah got residency on campus and Jessica found a room to rent near her college. They were beginning the journey into adulthood.

My friends visited with me the day before the first start of classes. Khadijah told me, "Be strong, life is too short to waste time." She hugged me for more than a moment and went home to prepare for school.

Jessica turned to me and smiled, she hugged me tightly. She told me, "I wish I could help you more boo. I want you to know, this too shall pass." Hearing these words gave me a slight warm feeling in the pit of my stomach, I felt butterflies again. "Start doing something you love, I'll see you soon. Love you girl." She grabbed her sweater from a chair in my room next to my bed and gave me a smile before leaving. And just like that, Jessica moved on to the next chapter in her life. I cried that night, my friends moved on, I was not the same, not moving forward with them.

I had a dream that night. I did not remember it well but I know I dreamt of Gabe and I know I felt calm and I felt loved. I do recall him saying something along the lines of *"You don't need to struggle, life can be easy if you want it to be."*

In the morning, I felt different, eager and ready to take on the day with enthusiasm. A weight had lifted off my chest, it felt like when a cold finally heals, when the stuffy nose becomes clear and you can breathe again. I got ready for the day, put on light jeans and a bright orange top; I felt like wearing vibrant colours today. I did my hair in braids, I was on a mission. I went downstairs and I could smell breakfast coming from the kitchen. Every morning has been like this, mom has been cooking my favourite foods to try and cheer me up. The smell reminded me of Noah so I didn't usually feel like eating, but today was different. Today I felt hungry and excited, and for once I felt happiness in smelling breakfast and being reminded of Noah.

'Morning mom.'

My mom looked at me wide eyed, "Good Morning Anastasia, you look beautiful honey. You are glowing." Her face had a sense of relief starting to show, I could tell she was getting excited because she just started grinning, she placed a plate of food in front of me, it was scrambled eggs with a side of bacon and a small bowl of oatmeal to accompany it. She sat down at the table across from me looking expectantly.

I looked at her smiling, "Thank you mom, and thank you so much for all you do, I really appreciate you trying to cheer me up lately."

"Well of course Ana! Anything for my baby girl."

I ate the breakfast which tasted delicious, I think I barely ate anything while I was stuck in my depression, breakfast was amazing today. My palette for food was coming back.

Once I was done eating, I looked up at my mom.

"Mom, can you take me to the garden store today? I would like to try something new. Do you mind if I do some work out in the backyard? I want to add a garden."

My mom grabbed her keys and called upstairs to my dad, "Honey, Ana and I are going to the garden center, be right back." She was enthusiastic and seemed ready to take me anywhere I asked.

We got to the garden center, as mom turned off the car, I looked at her and said, "Mom, I know I haven't been myself lately but I have a project in mind and I am hoping that maybe you could help me get everything I need today? I'd like to build a garden, I want to have fruits and vegetables, probably herbs too. Don't worry this will save you money in the long run." I grinned at her.

Mom looked at me, "Do you know what you are doing though? I mean, it's like farming, this takes a lot of work and dedication and the way you have been acting lately does concern me a bit. Are you ready for this kind of commitment?"

I understood what she meant; I didn't blame her for feeling this way. I had been lost for months. "Mom, I want you to know that I understand why you feel this way but I promise you, this is something I need to do and want to do. Also, I am going to grab a job application when we leave so I can afford this project and pay you and dad back for the supplies."

My mom looked at me, she seemed a bit teary eyed, but I think it was out of happiness or relief, either way she told me, "Baby girl, you don't owe me a cent for today. I support you and love you, don't ever forget it." We hugged and got out of the vehicle.

We left the store with a mountain of supplies: some wood to make the border of my garden, soil, vegetable seeds, strawberry seeds, raspberry seeds and multiple herbs. I had my work cut out for me, but I had a plan and determination to accomplish something that reminded me of my past and love for Noah.

When I got home my dad and brothers were waiting for me on the porch. They hugged me. Dad said, "I'm glad you're smiling sweetie. I love you, don't ever forget it."

"Thank you dad, I love you too. I am going to need your help though." He held me in his arms and we smiled at each other.

He headed towards the vehicle, "Come on boys, let's help your sister get started." My little brothers seemed enthusiastic to get their hands on the soil. We all started unloading the supplies and got to work on my garden.

Over the next year I worked on my garden, I got a job at the garden center and I worked as much as I could. I was determined to have the garden flourish and I was saving as much money as I could as well.

Jessica and Khadijah would come by and visit me when they had time between studies. I love them so much, they came over to help tend my garden with me at times and every so often we would meet up at the cinema to watch a movie or go on activities like mini putting and bowling. When they needed me, I would visit them at school and encourage them to keep going, keep studying, some days school was exceptionally tough and I didn't like my girls being stressed, so I would bring a care package usually made up of essential oils and soothing lotions or bath salts to help ease their pain.

Within the year Jessica changed her mind on what she was studying and applied for different courses. We were there for each other mentally and physically. We did not judge each other, we loved each other, and I was so grateful for these ladies in my life.

There was no more pressure or expectations, I could tell my parents were content with what I was doing with my life and did not seem worried at all. They told me they were confident I would make good decisions for myself and we would sometimes have dinner discussions to see what I may be interested in learning to start a full-time career. I was feeling more mature to start thinking about what might be practical for me in my professional future.

Two years had passed, my garden was flourishing. I grew zucchini, tomatoes, cucumbers, peppers, I had a raspberry bush growing next to the fence and a strawberry bush.

In summer, I harvested my garden, put some of the fresh fruit and veggies in a basket that I left inside the house for mom and loaded up the car with the rest.

I headed to a local church that gives food to those in need. Derek, an older man who helps run the program was standing outside the church waiting for me. "Ana, it's so good to see you." He said with a smile.

"Hey Derek, it's great to see you too. Such a beautiful day, right? Check out how much we were able to get this year."

Derek looked in the car and was extremely pleased with the amount of food I was able to provide for the food drive. "Ana, I really don't know what we would do without you, we can provide healthy, quality food because of people like you. Thank you so much for your contribution, it is greatly appreciated." I smiled and we started to unload the car.

When I got home, mom was in the kitchen cooking dinner, dad and my brothers were wrestling in the living room. "Mom, dad I'm home." I dropped my keys on the table next to the door. I went in the kitchen to join my mom and started helping by slicing peppers.

"Mom, I have been saving up money since I started working and now, I think I am ready to do some travelling."

Mom stopped cooking for a moment, "Ok sweetie, dad and I will look up locations and travel plans with you tonight. You know I hate to let you go alone but something tells me you got this. That being said, we will be booking with an agent to keep this adventure as safe as possible ok?"

I smiled, "Ok mom, your rules on this one will be fine by me."

That night, mom and dad helped me set up all my travel plans. I was going to take a plane to France, then to Italy and end the trip in Greece. I wanted to see some of my favourite places again.

Chapter 12

<hr>

I set off on my journey a few weeks later. I was excited; I was happy and proud of myself. I had made some of my dreams come true and I had help from my loved ones along the way.

I couldn't help but regularly think of Noah, all we went through and everything we did together on our travels. I decided to take pictures of every place we had once been and visited or close to it, as it was hard to pinpoint where I was, the land now looked completely different. Sometimes based on hills or mountains I might be able to recall us being there, but now the houses were all different and it was crowded. I wanted to have keepsakes of the places Noah and I had been together, even if it all was just a dream, I did not want to forget.

The days in France passed slowly, time was still. I finally felt a sense of freedom that I had missed and was craving. I took meditation classes with the top gurus and

I was practicing yoga just about every other day. I felt content for once. I met new friends and I lived like every day was my last.

When I made it to Italy I stopped at the location where I thought Lorenzo and I used to live. It looked completely different, there were no more vast, open farm lands or animals, it was now the main streets of Naples with roads and rows of homes built together. It is still beautiful, nonetheless. I was looking around at all the buildings, monuments and street art that had been created over the years, and I knew, even though I missed the world of my dreams, it did not have all this culture and history.

It was becoming clear to me, even though the world of my dreams had no strife and all the people lived in peace and prosperity we were missing the pain and evil which could give birth to some of the most beautiful things. Like, how an artist can take an empty canvas and use their emotions or pain and put it all on display for everyone to see and interpret for themselves and possibly inspire them to appreciate life.

One day, as I was walking through the marketplace buying food, I came across one man's stall who was selling cheese and fresh tomatoes; the aroma was wonderful. Something had drawn me closer. The man at the counter was dealing with a customer. I realized I knew him. "Can I help you?", I heard a familiar voice say. My heart stopped for a moment and I started to blush.

"Uh, yes. Um, do you have any samples of the cheese?", I felt like such an idiot. I wondered if there would be a glimmer of him ever remembering me and our flock of sheep and fresh fruit. I almost turned around to quickly walk away and never look back, I was terribly mortified, there's no way he would ever know we had once met.

To my surprise, he gave me the biggest smile and said, "I feel like I know you from somewhere. You seem very familiar," he gave me a very curious look, paused a moment and shook his head "but I know this is the first time we have met. That must seem strange to you, my name is Lorenzo and you are?" his accent was gorgeous, he reached out his hand to touch mine. I responded by handing my hand in his to shake it. I know there was a spark.

My heart skipped again, he must have remembered me! I couldn't believe it, so many thoughts started racing through my mind, all the things we did together, oh gosh, my mind kept telling me not to blush. "I am Anastasia and I agree with you, there is definitely something familiar here." *Idiot* I thought. I sounded like a complete moron. In my mind I was laughing at myself. *Pull yourself together Ana* I thought.

"Where are you from? Are you travelling with anyone?", he looked slightly over my shoulder to see if anyone was following me.

"I am from Canada, travelling on my own currently. Exploring parts of the world I feel connected to. I'll be around for a little bit before heading over to Greece." I know it is not smart at all to tell a complete stranger that you are alone in a foreign country and I highly suggest a young lady never does that, but I knew him. It was my Lorenzo.

I started to feel confident in my words, it felt easy to speak to him.

"Well, if you are interested, I can show you around. I'll show you the best spots in town to eat and drink to your heart's desire." He was smiling so sweetly; I had not realized how much I missed him too. After all, Lorenzo was my first love in my dream world. I owed it to myself to explore this relationship now.

"I would love that, when do you finish work?" I said.

He turned to an older gentleman who I think was his father, he had the same smile and frown lines in his forehead as Lorenzo did. They exchanged some words in Italian, his father looked at me and smiled approvingly, nodded at Lorenzo to go and he grabbed my hand excited to show me around.

The next couple of days Lorenzo and I were inseparable. He would meet me early every morning, sometimes greeting me with flowers or fresh fruit. It was such a beautiful gesture. I was happy to know that no matter what world we lived in, Lorenzo was always a good person.

He took me out every evening; we danced, drank wine, ate great food and even had dinner with his father. His father told us many stories of his youth and how Naples had changed over the years, we laughed and drank into the night. He took me around the countryside and told me all about the area and its history. There were beautiful stories and dark ones. We enjoyed every moment together. I took as many photos as I could, but I kept having to remind myself to take photos because I was having too much fun and living in the moment. Lorenzo was sweet enough to pick up the camera a few times for me and take photos of parts he thought I should remember. We even had passers by take photos of us together.

On my last day, like clockwork, Lorenzo was waiting for me in the lobby. I could see that Lorenzo was somber; I felt sad too. I had finally met a familiar face, someone who was once my first love, but this time it was different. There were more obstacles to overcome this time. We both lived in different countries, and we couldn't just take off in the wind and be together in harmony. I understood this and I was prepared to say goodbye as I had done it once before.

Lorenzo looked me in the eyes, "Anastasia, these days have been wonderful for me. I feel like we have known each other for such a long time. I don't know if I am being too forward but I do feel love for you. A love like I have not felt before. I must say that I do not want this to end. I want you to stay with me forever, but something tells me this may be it for now."

I was flattered and I knew what he was talking about, I felt it too, "Lorenzo, I feel the same. Why not stay inside for the day? Say our goodbyes in the most memorable way possible."

We grinned at each other, "I think that sounds like a good idea." He kissed me softly, on the lips, but the softness turned to passion. We went to my hotel room and we didn't leave all day.

The next day I had to catch my plane to Greece, I awoke to a soft kiss on my forehead, Lorenzo and I were naked in each other's arms. We made love one last time, then I packed and he took me to the Airport. As he put my bags down he looked up at me teary eyed and held my hands in his, "I promised myself I wouldn't cry but your love is very powerful. Anastasia, you have such a beautiful soul and I am so glad I had these moments with you. I hope that one day you may come back looking for me. I truly wish you didn't have to leave."

I had butterflies, part of me didn't want to leave him either but I was content in knowing that he was doing well and we got to meet again. "Lorenzo, you have no idea how happy I am to have gotten the chance to meet you again. I know it seems strange but I have loved you before, you can believe it or not but I do love you. I don't know what our future holds but know that I wish you all the best in whatever may come next. You have made this adventure more special than I could ever imagine." I gave him a kiss, we hugged and I grabbed my bags, took one last look at Lorenzo and proceeded in the airport.

I had one last week before going home. Greece was beautiful and exciting, I danced, met fellow travellers and partied like a rock star. I knew this would be my last vacation for a while, I knew once I got home, I would need to get serious about school.

Chapter 13

◆—◆—◆

After a long and joyous trip I was excited to go home. When I got home my family was happy to see me. After a day of rest my parents took my brothers and I out to the beach for a day trip, we ate whatever we wanted: ice cream, poutine, burgers and we did lots of swimming. It was fun. Everything was becoming more and more clear to me: I was starting to understand how to navigate this life. I felt I had some control back, like I could live a full and happy life and still deal with the responsibilities that come with it.

Once in a while I did have moments when I felt down, but I realized that this was normal and, as long as I had a plan in place, I could bounce back from feeling sad or empty. I had a routine which consisted of regular exercise, eating as healthy as I could (aside from the bowl of ice cream here and there; I mean you only live once right?), I would also do yoga and meditate every day or so. I started to feel satisfied, similar to how I felt as a child and similar to how I felt in the life I once had.

As time went on, I finally applied for school, I decided to study social economics. For fun, I made videos of myself gardening and teaching others how to create their own dream garden.

One day, near the end of summer, I was tending my garden in the backyard. I was listening to music with headphones, dancing around, and watering the plants. I felt someone come up behind me. My mom tapped my shoulder. I jumped, startled. I took out my headphones and swung around, "Mom! You scared me!" I started laughing at myself, and at that moment I noticed him standing there, smiling at me.

My mom said, "Ana, you have company, this is Noah he said you may remember him from school? Anyways I'll let you two catch up." She gave me a smile and walked slowly to the house, probably to try and listen to our conversation but eventually went through the side door.

I don't think my heart was beating at all in that moment, that or it was beating so fast I didn't notice because I was overwhelmed to see him standing right there before me.

"Ana, do you...", he started to speak and I ran and jumped into his arms. He caught me and we started laughing. We kissed passionately and time stood still.

We embraced, we did not want to let go, afraid it would end again. I took his hand and led him to the tree, our tree, and talked. Noah couldn't keep his eyes off me, "Ana I wasn't sure if you would still be here, or if you would even remember. I want to say something to you, I've been wanting to say this to you for years... I love you. I hope you know I always did and my decision to come back had nothing to do with me wanting to leave you. I just knew I had to see this life through, I wanted to become the man you deserved. I want you to be my forever and I wanted to be strong for you, and also for myself. I needed to find myself to be with you." He stopped and looked at me intently, searching my eyes for an answer or comment to what he had to say.

"Noah, I was broken when you left, I really was. I couldn't see the light, but I picked myself up and accomplished so much in this time. I always had you in my heart and I came to understand why it was right for us to come back, this made me a better person, I understand so much more now." I paused for a moment to look at his eyes and touch his cheek to confirm I was not dreaming. "I am so happy you came for me. You are my person in this crazy world. I love you, for now, for always, forever."

Author's Letter

Dear Reader,

I would like to say thank you for reading this story. I hope in some way, parts of the story resonated with you. It took me time and care to put this together and release it to the world to enjoy.

I believe one of the key messages of this story, is to encourage you to try and live your life judgement free. I want you to be able to feel the freedom Anastasia felt when she transitioned into the other reality, the reality of freedom from judgement and guilt. I want you to be able to take the feeling of satisfaction with you for the rest of your life and genuinely enjoy every moment you can.

I appreciate the support and positive feedback from the community. I encourage you to lead with love, even in the darkest of times, as they too shall pass, and I encourage you to reach out to your inner child, remember the activities that bring you joy, and try to implement that into your life today. Take your time and enjoy the process.

Sincerely,

Kayla Smickle